DINOSAUR DINOSAUR

Kevin Lewis

Illustrated by Daniel Kirk

SCHOLASTIC PRESS

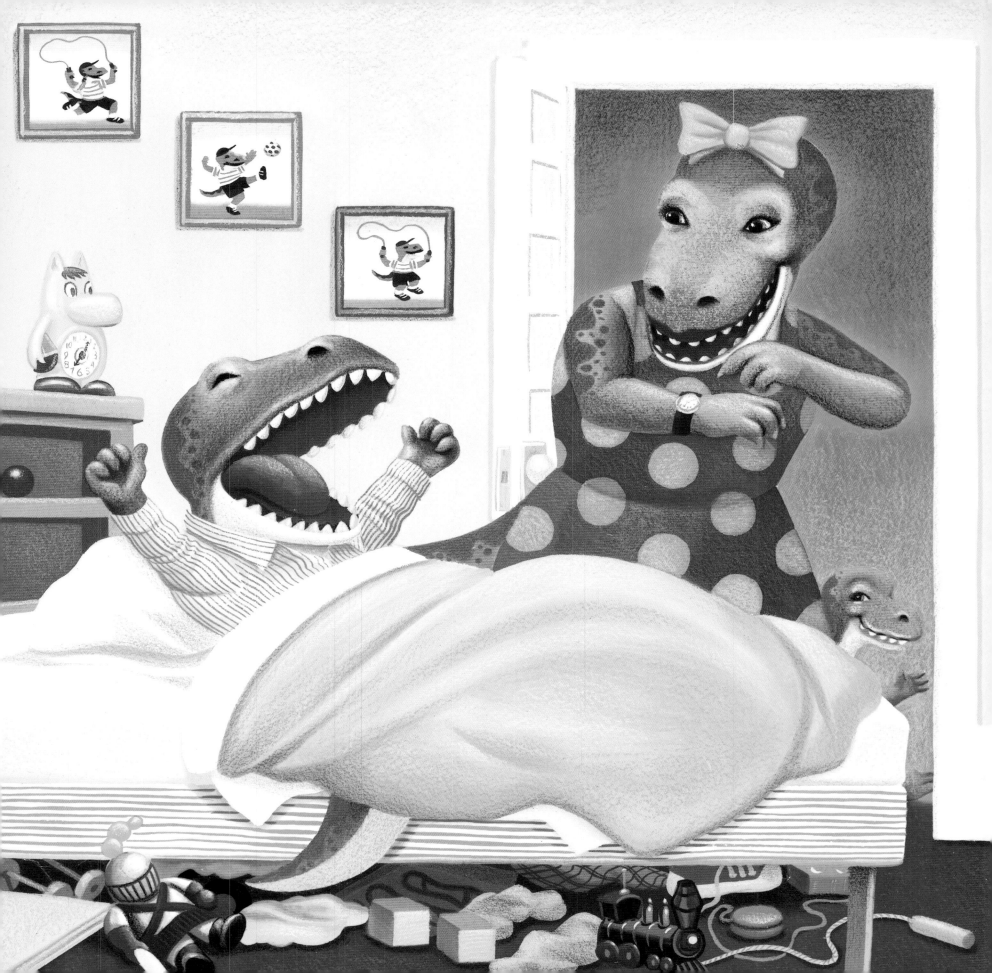

Dinosaur, dinosaur,
wake up with a roar!
Grumpy-lumpy dinosaur,
stomp across the floor!

Yummy-tummy dinosaur,
sit right down to eat.
Munchy-crunchy dinosaur,
what a breakfast treat!

Dinosaur, dinosaur,
all those teeth to brush.
Pacy-racy dinosaur,
dressing in a rush!

Ready-freddy dinosaur.
But where's your other shoe?
Looky-looky, dinosaur,
it's playing peekaboo!

Jumpy-bumpy dinosaur,
run outside and play.
Busy-whizzy dinosaur...

...all the livelong day!

Dinosaur, dinosaur,
laughing without care.
Funny-bunny dinosaur,
hopping everywhere!

Happy-yappy dinosaur,
running all around.

Bouncy-pouncy dinosaur,
till the sun is going down.

Dinosaur, dinosaur,
please don't run and hide!
Itsy-bitsy dinosaur,
time to go inside.

Howly-yowly dinosaur,
look, the stars are out!
Tiny-whiny dinosaur,
there's no need to pout.

Dinosaur, dinosaur,
messy as can be.
Slurpy-burpy dinosaur,
come and dine with me.

Muddy-duddy dinosaur,
soap up in the tub.
Bubbly-wubbly dinosaur,
rub-a-dub-a-dub.

Dinosaur, dinosaur,
what a sleepyhead,
Huffing-puffing dinosaur,
now it's time for bed!

Cosy-dozy dinosaur,
let's turn off the light.
I love you, little dinosaur,
good night . . .

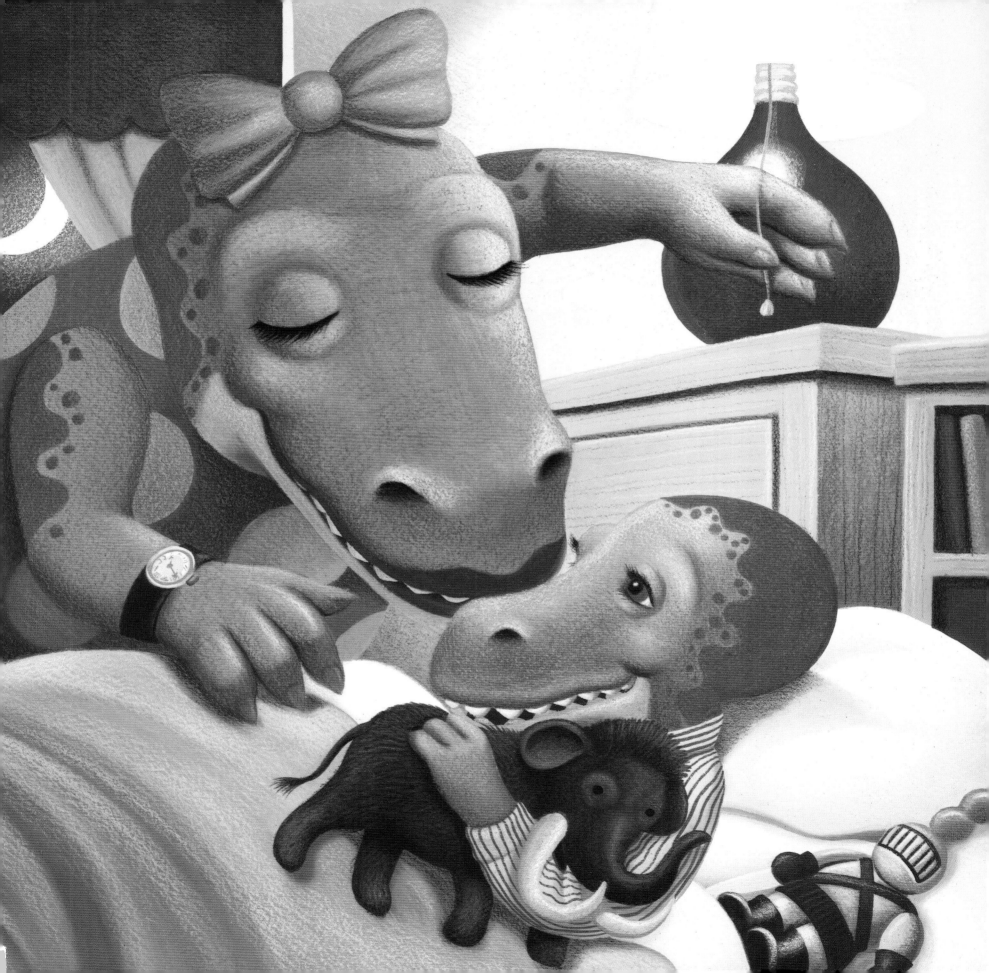

. . . sleep tight!